CITIES

CITIES

Elizabeth Thorpe

*t*P
Texture Press
2016

Published in the United States by
Texture Press
Managing Editor: Susan Smith Nash, Ph.D.
1108 Westbrooke Terrace
Norman, OK 73072
Email: texturepress@beyondutopia.com

For ordering information,
visit the Texture Press website at
www.texturepress.org

Cover and book design by Arlene Ang
Cover photo by Elizabeth Thorpe

ISBN-13: 978-0-692-66286-1
ISBN-10: 0-692-66286-3

For my parents

*We stood above the highway, taillights
like rubies on the curve of a neck. The city
a gift you gave me, one I wouldn't wear.*

· TABLE OF CONTENTS ·

Port Townsend

In the place of ghosts. Lines of rooms with light switches on the outside, reverberation of shouted orders, toe to heel, brass pins pinned straight on thick wool uniforms. Rooms that housed the broken ones, the frightened ones. The ones tucking packs of cigarettes under their mattresses. The ones smudging the ink on letters from their mothers. The ones drawing pictures in the margins, of breasts, of racecars, of the freighters passing through the channel they see blurred through salt-stained windows.

At night, the spray of stars over the parade grounds, the tall trees bobbing and weaving in the wind, the bell buoy clanging *lonely, lonely, lonely.* A cruise ship lit up huge and silent, rounding the point of the lighthouse, the lighthouse big and then small and then big again. Beyond, the bunkers pitchdark-silent, graffiti on their inner walls, swastikas and peace signs.

Ghost of touch on skin, a hair rising in a follicle. Ghost of dew soaking into clothes, ghost of *would kissing you make it better or worse?* Ghost of not good enough, not brave enough, not special. Ghost of *what does it matter?* Vapor of words read slow, hypnotic, of words read wild-eyed, of words the mouth won't open wide enough to say. The ghost-body sea glass, rolled again and again through rocks bigger and stronger, all sides diminished.

We return to the place of ghosts, hard yellow grass poking through our shoes, mist sweeping around the trim white buildings, crows on the picnic table fighting for trash. We return, and we are paint over paint over paint on a broad white deck. We are skin on flesh on bone.

"And The Future Is"

We bought the shoes together, while shopping at T.J. Maxx on a Friday night with Mandy's mom. I loved Mandy's mom, partly because she looked like Demi Moore in *Ghost*, but also because she was younger and cooler than my mom. My mom would have laughed if she saw the shoes, and also if she saw my bangs curled into a poofball by Mandy's mom the next morning (it had deflated by the time she came to pick me up). But Mandy's mom was used to things like this from Mandy. We put our money together to buy the shoes, but agreed that Mandy would have custody, because I didn't want my mom to laugh at me, and because Mandy's house had better floors for practicing our runway walks.

When we were eleven, Mandy was Debbie Gibson and Exclamation perfume and a tiny flower of a body that got heat rash when her parents grounded her and she had to stay inside one week that summer. She was a note-writer, a pink-pen user, a girl who used stars as punctuation.

But she was also born on Halloween, and dressed up as a sluttier witch every year. She bought me a Ouija board for my birthday when I was thirteen, then borrowed it the next year for a party I wasn't invited to and never gave it back. And then she was on drugs, and then she was pregnant, you know. You know.

In high school, Mr. Floyd said to never wear shoes you can't run in, and that's me now. Maybe it's partly because of Mandy, although I hardly ever think about her anymore. But when I see that peekaboo heel alone in the woods, I sit down in the wet leaves next to it, touch it gently like I touched Mandy's heat rash, keep it company for a while.

Offshore Winds

———

A sailboat with a crew of two, a childless couple who took us out with them sometimes, me and my brother, motoring out through fluorescent buoys and rowboats at rest, waiting for the lobstermen to make their way back across early morning, the wide spread of sunlight across flat calm like a glass tabletop in the type of store my parents didn't like to let my brother go in. A kid who crashed, who kept his head down and rammed my shoulder, knocking me onto the dirt road on the way to the bus stop, on a morning I didn't want to be awake, a morning when I would watch the way the sun fell into the woods – sun on leaves, then birch bark, boulder, moss – and wish I could follow it all day. Tracking light instead of seats on a bus, chalk on a board. Today we were on the ocean, weaving among moorings like I wove floss into bracelets that summer, one end pinned near the knee of my jeans, hands moving, calm despite my brother freewheeling around me. And for an hour he was calm too, leaning back on the deck, looking up at the sails.

Skin

She had never noticed the freckle above her lover's navel. Not until that afternoon, as he lay on the bed with his shirt pulled up, humidity-sweat dried by the fan's weak breeze. How had she never noticed? Maybe she had and forgot, and she wondered what else she had forgotten, what peculiarities of other lovers' bodies.

She wondered if mothers forgot or if they memorized every inch of their babies' clean, unbroken planes of skin and remembered them always. How would it be to be a mother and see a beloved child's skin pierced, reddened, by jewelry? Or inked by tattoos or broken by misfortune? How would it be to rush a child's compound fracture to the hospital, seeing the bright white bone no one was ever meant to see, laid out like a myth, an excavation, to be studied and reburied changed, documented, no longer a secret?

What would it be like to let a child grow up and go away to a lover who would know the adult body better than a mother ever could?

A treasure, this body, the skin that she alone viewed, she and he together and separately and daily. How could she not notice, but then how could she? It was impossible to live on the plane of the first flush of love, when lovers sat at each other's tables and devoured the details of each other. After that first feast, they took the crumbs of details as they came: summer hair brightened by sunlight, knees that ached in movie theaters, skin pulled tight over shoulder bones. And the way these things changed.

On Vacation

They're not talking much. The crabgrass is rough on her feet. Sheets snap on the line, billow, go slack. Seaweed clings to the anchor line. She forgets to put sunscreen on her stomach, and burns. She soaks in the claw-foot bathtub. The bell buoy clangs. On the wall is a mural of evergreens.

She reads a book about diving horses at Coney Island. He fishes for mackerel. They don't mow their lawn. The grass grows as high as the swing seats.

The sky is so dark the window is a mirror. With no TV the nights stretch long. Rain on the roof. Foghorn. Wind. She scrapes fish scales off the plates.

The couch is stiff. Her feet are cold, he does not warm them.

The windjammers flock into the hot harbor. They watch from the deck. His beer sweats. She pulls her hair off her neck. Clean white sails, free of dirt. For a moment, she is buoyed.

Adolescence

The barn burned in January, on a night cold as shattered glass, a night when you could see stars between the stars. It didn't mean much to anybody anymore. Farley had sold off most of his land, and the barn was left to itself, sliding down from its roof-ridge, the ridge twisting like the back of an old man. The inside was full of broken things, things that might be worth saving but weren't worth keeping in the attic or the basement and cats that were wild and not worth keeping inside, either.

The barn meant nothing to anybody anymore except for me and maybe Jed. Jed must have cared about it once, I think, but I don't know if he still does. He's not the sentimental type, not like me. Maybe he doesn't even remember anymore, the hot bored afternoons when we went in there together and he wrestled me down on the floor and I pretended to fight back but didn't try too hard. Every afternoon I felt the weight of him, more and more solid and dry and warm as the summer went on. We lay there on the pine boards, still and saying nothing, and then after a while, always after not long enough, he would get up and I would get up and he would run off somewhere and I'd try not to follow.

Boyfriends: A Mixtape

1. "Just Like Jesse James"
Each finger brushed against the thumb, her hands curling into fists. "Can I carry your backpack?" Peter says. "Do you want to be my girlfriend?" The worst thing is she does. She wants to be someone's girlfriend, wants it so badly. She wants to sit with a boy on the way back from basketball games, bus dark, radio on, coaches way up in the front near the driver. But his friends are laughing. It's just a joke, or a trick. She doesn't know what to do except stand there, hands at her sides, wait for him to give up and go away. The classroom smells chemical, like dry-erase markers and the hard new carpets they just put in.

Peter reaches his hand out, reaches his left hand toward her right, and she can almost feel the heat of his skin, and she wishes this could be real. She turns away, and Peter says, "You don't want to go out with me?" He says it like he's hurt, but she knows he's not, and his friends are laughing, and she just wants the bell to ring for recess. It's October, getting cold, the ground hard. She's wearing a skirt because there's a game tonight and they have to dress up when there's a game. But maybe when she gets outside she will sit on the hill, maybe she will lie back like she used to last year, imagine the flying machine she will build with boxes and balloons. The machine rising with her in it, into the blue October sky. She tries to imagine that instead of what she knows will happen later: she will sit on the bus alone, closer to the front than the back, she will look at her reflection in the cold windows and listen to someone on the radio singing about love.

2. "Everybody Hurts"
"None of that is important now that I'm with you," he says. "Everything is important."

They are driving through open farmland, in a place where the kids get a month off in the fall to help with the potato harvest. He has recently started college in a town where the roads are pink from pink granite and the people willfully ignore the French pronunciation of their town's name, preferring a Downeast broadness. The sky is overcast, which makes the fall colors on the few trees look brighter.

He has been asked to speak at a conference involving educators from across the state. His speech is about the benefits of a vocational education, specifically culinary arts. They are the youngest people there. Her tights are too short, and keep rolling down her hips. She tries not to pull at them. He starts his speech with a joke about how the town is so small that the soap just says "Di". She wrote the essay that got him this scholarship, and she thinks she should have helped with his speech too. She would have told him to use Dove soap as an example instead of Dial. As he continues, she looks at his tie (too short, too wide), at his Doc Martens with the bright yellow stitches, and she imagines the older people thinking, "this is the best we could do?"

This is what she is starting to think, it's what she thinks while they're having sex in the shower in their first hotel room, but she won't admit it to anyone. This is the man she will marry. They will have a house and two children, a boy and a girl. She is seventeen, but she has already started her real life.

3. "The Last Worthless Evening"
Sun punctuates every corner. Monday afternoon and she is driving back home from college, driving to meet him at the Dunkin Donuts that marks halfway. The sun is low in the trees, she blinks and blinks as it glares and recedes. Her eyes are tired of crying. Her hands are cold on the steering wheel.

It's not the weekend, and she doesn't belong here. At school, everyone is just going to dinner, lining up to pack their trays with pizza, cereal, mashed potatoes and gravy from a box and a jar, apple juice and chocolate milk and Mountain Dew. If she stopped at her parents' house they would fix her a better dinner, make something she loves. If she stopped, they would know. They would worry.

By the time she crests the hill, it's dark enough to see the lights of town on the horizon. They are coals in a fireplace, near exhausted. She knows that when he sees her, everything will be different. She will be with him tonight, and tomorrow she will drive back to where she's supposed to be. Nothing matters more than this.

His car is on the far edge of the parking lot. Exhaust rises into the cold. How many times has she met him here? In shorts and t-shirts, in winter coats, with skis, with tents, with roses, in black night and early morning, on dark days when the rain drips through the corner of his windshield and runs down to the dash. Now she parks beside him, takes a breath before she opens her door. She looks up to see if the stars are out, but the lights of the parking lot are too bright for her to tell. She gets in. His car smells of coffee – French vanilla in her cup holder, covered and waiting, the flavor marked in Sharpie on the cover. She smiles to see it. It's all okay now.

"You're making it worse," he says.

4. "Box of Rain"
She sleeps on a study lounge couch her friends have dragged into their dorm room, curled into a cave of forgetting. They listen to a meditation tape to fall asleep, something Justin got when he was a swimmer in high school. It goes through the

motions, stroke, stroke, turn, breathe, sounds becoming familiar as home.

They all squeeze into the back of a station wagon to smoke pot and listen to *Before These Crowded Streets* in its entirety on the radio, the day before its release.

They walk at night behind the dorm, shuffling through powdered snow, and in the trees' long shadows she sees wolves, but she is not afraid.

Back inside, Justin makes grilled cheese sandwiches in his toaster oven and she is content in the room that smells of men with whom she will never have sex, although one night when Justin is away she will climb into Paul's bed and he will hold her close against his wide hairless chest while they both think of his girlfriend sleeping 600 miles away. In the morning, she will wear his soccer shorts back to the girls' wing, and the next night she will be back on their couch, her couch, and Justin will never know.

5. "I'll Back You Up"
He's this guy she works with at the bookstore. He wears a battered Yankees hat to staff meetings and gets to leave early every day for baseball practice. He's a year younger, and she has a crush on his best friend.

But then there's a night when they're all skating out on the lake, playing tag in the dark, and he swoops in close and reaches out but doesn't tag her. And then there's a chilly night when they all go play mini golf and she wears his sweatshirt, which smells sweet, like the kind of laundry detergent her mom will never buy. And then they both close the store on a night near Christmas, and he surprises her with a gift – a Bela Fleck and the Flecktones CD. Several days later she gives him the widescreen VHS tape of *Armageddon*, because she knows he likes Owen Wilson.

Now it's New Year's Eve, and they're in a friend's basement. She's sitting on the dirty stairs, and a couple of people are playing ping pong, and then he picks up a three-quarter sized guitar with three strings, and starts playing, well enough for her to recognize the song.

Dirigo

Yard sales on tables made of scrap wood and sawhorses. Baked bean suppers and pancake breakfasts and turkey shoot fundraisers. Camo and hunter orange and waders and mud, wet dogs and sheepskin slippers and flip flops and Muck boots. Lobster boats pulling away from their dinghies in the cold, clean air, diesel motors and fluorescent lines and stacks of wire mesh traps. Flannel and denim and down. A Styrofoam cup of Dunkin, steam rising. Seeing your breath, mist over the lake as it cools and thickens. The boom of ice as it settles, standing out in the middle on crunchy snow, a bowl of stars above. Pine trees and balsam pillows and blueberry jam, lobster stew and popovers. A basketball game in a junior high gym, sneakers squeaking, the smell of a popcorn machine, little kids thundering up and down the wooden bleachers. A casserole made with five kinds of Campbell's soup. Walmart blouses and coolers and bike pumps and plant pots. Beans planted in the spring, stakes with cakes of Ivory soap on top to keep the deer away. Shivering in the front seat next to your boyfriend, taking one mitten off to hold his hand. A walk on the train tracks, balancing on one metallic tie, arms out for balance. Greeting cards and knick knacks and potpourri under vacuum tracks, houses that smell of scented candles matched to the season: pumpkin, Christmas wreath, sugar cookie, lilac, sea breeze. Stopping by and dropping in and calling the landline, leaving each other alone, knowing everyone's business. The way the plastic snaps off a stack of the *New York Times* when it gets to the bookstore on Sundays. Camp chairs and campfires, woodstoves and wooden toys. The way low tide smells like a bonfire on the wind from far away. Super glue and Elmer's glue and Shoe Goo, fixing things you can't stand to throw away. A Red Sox sweatshirt with the hood tipped up to keep sunset's chill off your neck. Standing alone in the woods at night, wind in the trees like a freight train, the moon obscured by clouds, and then clear.

The Bridesmaid

I had to go and get a bridesmaid's dress at David's Bridal in the suburbs. It was going to be dark purple, one of our high school's colors, although the bride wouldn't admit it. To her, it was Lapis, and there was a difference. I had to shave my legs and wear a nice-looking bra and go in there and get a short satin Lapis-colored dress and bring in my shoes from Payless that I needed to have dyed to match. I had to do it today, because the wedding was only a month away. They would need to alter the dress to fit me.

I shaved my legs and wore the bra and took the shoes and got in the car, started it and let it run for a while, because it had been so long since we'd moved it. I left our parking spot and drove through our neighborhood to the outskirts of the city, to where I had to get on the highway that would shoot me out to the suburbs. But before I got to the on-ramp for the highway I stopped. I was in this neighborhood I'd never been in before. And I had to get to David's Bridal before they closed early because it was Sunday, so I didn't have time to screw around, but I stopped the car and turned it off and I got out and I walked, arms crossed, the breeze cold on my face. I walked by a place that sold pulled-pork sandwiches and had a neon sign that was an outline of a pig. And I walked by an Irish pub with big-bellied guys standing in the doorway smoking and I turned down a different street and walked by some antique stores that were closed and a store that had big bolts of fabric leaned up against the inside of the window, which had a gate pulled down over it in case someone wanted to smash it.

And I stopped in front of this other antique store with a black and white picture of a family in a parade. The sun beat down on them so they could just look up a little bit, under their hats. And this blond kid with the word Mexico stitched on his hat was sitting on a mule painted to look like a zebra, disguised as something it was clearly not. And everyone around it was smiling.

Apnea

At night she dreams of wet passageways. She dreams the smell of wet iron, the beam of her flashlight shining on wall after wall, moving forward with no promise of an end. She wakes and wakes.

She has promised Carl that when she goes home she will see the doctor. Carl worries. He says sometimes he lies awake and listens to her sleep, wills her to start breathing again, wonders if he should wake her and remind her to breathe. Carl sleeps warm against her, and sometimes the warmth loosens the strained muscles in her back, and sometimes she just wants to shake him off like a heavy blanket, although it gets so cold in the tents late at night. Maybe she sleeps fine, breathes fine, in her bed at home. She doesn't remember ever waking so often.

Every day the sun streams down as they crouch and pick, brush and blow the dust around. From time to time she looks up at the cloudless sky, tries to rest her eyes. She wishes she could see the sky pure blue, without the little hairs and bits of dust floating in her eye fluid. She wants something that simple.

Coke

My brother and I sat on stumps in our neighbor's driveway, stumps that were the bright damp flesh color that meant they'd just been cut. We'd been out for a walk with our dad. Clear October, perfect blue sky. Saturday sounds ringing across the lake: an ax splitting firewood, a woodpecker hammering into a tree, someone's dog barking, which made our puppy bark too. It was already too cold for waterskiiers and jetskiiers, so the only motor sounds were Frankie's saw and the cars far off on Route 1-A.

Frankie lived halfway to the end of the road where I waited for the bus on school days. We had turned down his driveway to say hi, and now we were sitting and watching him talk to our dad about cutting wood, about winterizing. This morning I had decided that my favorite word was "preparations", as in "we are making our preparations for the winter." I had been helping my dad by pulling firewood around in my red plastic wagon and keeping Sam occupied and away from Dad while Dad used the ax.

I leaned back and looked up at the sky ringed with yellow leaves and brown leaves, a few green leaves still. Frankie asked Dad if he wanted a beer, and Dad said sure, and I knew that it would be Budweiser and Dad only drank Budweiser to be polite. Dad didn't like American beer too much, so every time we went to England he brought back malt extract and hops and yeast, a big metal keg one time. We helped our dad with his beer brewing, too. We helped him fill the bucket with water from the bathtub and we listened to the beer bubbling in the secondary and we complained about the smell like our mom did and we said "what color! What texture!" when Dad held up one of his pint glasses from England, showed us the way the light shone through the finished beer.

That morning Frankie came out with a beer for Dad and a Coke for me and my brother to share. We'd never had soda before. It wasn't like we weren't allowed, or anything, we just never had it in the house. Sam cracked it open after two tries and he took the first sip, more like a glug, and he slobbered so I had to pull the sleeve of my flannel shirt down over my hand and wipe the can before I took my sip. I tipped some back and it hurt, the fizz was hard on my mouth and the taste was hard too. Sam grabbed it back and took another big glug, and I didn't know if I even wanted any more, so I let Sam keep it for a while.

The air smelled like sawdust and dead leaves and gas from Frankie's chainsaw and smoke from Frankie's woodstove. I ran my fingers along the bark on the side of the stump. I looked at Frankie's feet and my dad's feet. Frankie wore dirty workboots that were kind of torn up. Dad wore the old sneakers he always used when he weed whacked the lawn. They had dried grass on them, and grass stains, and our puppy had chewed the Nike swoosh off one side. I elbowed Sam for no reason, just because, and he pushed me back a little until our dad looked down at us with his eyebrows frowning. Sam gave me the Coke back. It still hurt to drink it. I didn't like Coke, I decided. Coke was like Budweiser. I liked whatever was better.

"Don't Stop 'Til You Get Enough"

A highway attraction: South of the Border in South Carolina. 935 miles from Portland, Maine. 519 from Philadelphia. Fireworks store, sweet tea, a life-sized cactus made of fiberglass. The store is full of American flags and ashtrays shaped like sombreros. I buy a straw cowboy hat with red stitching across the brim. In front of the cactus in my straw hat I smile for pictures, showing the folks at home how happy I can still be. Being in motion makes me feel normal, as we make our way down the concrete highway to anywhere new. Anywhere that's never meant to be home.

Waffle Houses, Cracker Barrels, a Super 8 motel where it's warm enough to open the window at night in March. I make a careful list of states on the back of a brown paper bag, and we play the license plate game, checking off everything but Wyoming and Montana.

Pushed aside are the long lifeless days, the dread just after waking. I have a purpose, and it is to see everything. Michael Jackson plays on the radio and then in my head.

Savannah: trees draped with Spanish moss, pink and white blossoms bursting through the black ironwork, petals dripping on the sidewalk. Low Country Boil with peel-and-eat shrimp, little projects to busy the hands. Rain and rain and rain, singing in the gutters, patterning the river. We dry ourselves with paper towels in public restrooms.

Although I'm not religious, we attend an Easter service. When they play the pipe organ, the toccata my grandmother requested for her funeral, I feel it hard in my chest, in this city of ghosts.

That night on the hostel's veranda I watch the moss swing in the wind, signaling a new storm.

Emergency

1.

I board the bus that will take me to the train back to my city. The mist is still low, it's early morning. I try to name all the shades of green in the trees.

I stay awake until the bus crosses the bridge between this state and the next. When we were little, on our way to see our grandparents in Connecticut, we pushed our feet as far forward as they could go, under the seats – I'm in New Hampshire first! Then we threw our hands back – I'm in Maine last! As an adult, I feel only a thick dread, not wanting to cross.

The train ride from Boston – dry yellow grasses, pebbled gravestone, broken-windowed warehouse, stacked boxcars. The bridge that says "Trenton Makes the World Takes" in orange lights. Finally, my city's skyline, radio towers blinking red, Liberty One lit Eagle green, the Verizon building still tallest. Every new skyscraper has a company's name.

2.

The Comcast building is a hole in the ground behind the hotel where we live. I see it from our laundry room window, and I try to remember to take pictures of its progress, although I'm not sure why.

My grandfather made an album of a new building's progress in 1940. The album had thick black paper and the pictures were all black and white and small, two by three inches. My grandfather labeled the stages of the project in white pencil. That album was the one thing I gave away, donated to a museum in Hartford. It's the one thing I should have kept.

Sometimes traffic on the wet street sounds like ocean waves. From the hotel balcony I try to pick out stars in the humid sky. My hands palm the damp metal railing. "It's an emergency," a poet once told me, "that I'm not with you."

3.

I take an office job and spend my workdays studying the history of the building. Cold-storage Fur Vault (pictured: piles of skins with heads attached, buffalo hung high on a side wall, one eye on the camera). Pipe organ so large its pieces filled thirteen freight cars for its trip from St. Louis. Maine granite exterior, fashioned in the Roman-Doric style. The interior blanded now by a chain store – pipe organ playing patriotic favorites each noon, a thoroughbred held to a canter.

At night in the hotel I sit in a camping chair, feet on the radiator, reading biographies. I tell myself that I enjoy studying the arcs of whole lives, but really I am steeping in death. John Wanamaker with his 45-acre store, his fifty passenger elevators and Commercial Institute Military Band, gone like my grandparents, like that long-dead buffalo. What does it matter, happiness or misery, achievement?

4.

On days off I walk the city, trying to know it. Carpenters' Hall: history in a glass-fronted case, tools used to build a structure smaller than any modern McMansion. Chisel, file, spade, hung on pegs beside a sepia photograph of the work-in-progress. Wood shavings for decoration. I think of my parents' garage, the jumble of my grandfather's tools.

A little lightness when I notice things. Carved above the automatic door and below the lightbox sign of a drugstore: *hats trimmed free of charge*. I sit in the courtyard of the Rodin museum, reading and watching limbs of sycamores toss in a high breeze, sunlight on some leaves and then others.

5.

Afternoon light slants across the sidewalks of late summer. My yellow polo shirt is soaked with sweat as I walk home from my first day of another new job. One foot and then the other foot on the uneven red brick. The backpack pulls at the back of my shirt so I have to tug it down every few steps. Motion – I look up at the Victorian details at the tops of the row houses, at the way the light hits the paint. I'd see it differently from a car.

This is my life now. Backpack heavy with new free books, chalk in the cracks of the skin around my fingernails. Late summer and I'm not on a soccer field, not lining up to boot the ball toward the goal with new cleats on my feet. Late summer and I'm not walking up the dirt road to change from school clothes to sun-faded swimsuit. I'm not floating in an inner tube, watching the late light high in the trees, each leaf flapping distinct. One foot and then the other. I feel purpose, I feel history – great-grandmother, grandmother, grandfather, father, teachers all.

Brick gives way to concrete. Sun still hot enough to melt a Swedish fish, bleed its edges into the pavement ahead of me. I hitch my backpack up, pull the back of my shirt down. My classroom: rows of plastic/metal/wood desks, windows facing the buildings named after companies. Students who still raise their hands for permission to go to the bathroom. Others whose lives are newly aflame: Solo cups, vending machines, sunrises.

At home it's already fall, red leaves gather in construction sites named for nobody. My mother sorts through years of Halloween costumes so small she can't believe we ever wore them.

A siren comes close, gains momentum, then fades.

ENG 205

He was a hockey player from Montreal. He smoked pot in the woods behind the basketball hoops, just outside the ring of the dorm's orange light, with my friend Justin. Once Justin introduced him to me, and he said, yeah, I know her, though I never knew why. The class fulfilled a requirement for him, and most of the time he didn't speak, just nodded when the professor called his name for attendance. I sat there in the desk behind him, three days a week, looking at the way his dark hair curled, sometimes wet, sometimes dry and tangled, into the collars of his shirts, hockey hair. Sometimes he wore a bright blue sweater with big uneven stitches that looked homemade, and a collar that kind of rested low so you could see bare skin over the muscles in his neck.

Finally one day he had to read something in class. He looked down at the paper the whole time and read fast about Nintendo games lined up on the wooden shelf above his bed, the faded colors of the labels, how he prized them. The story ended when his basement room flooded and they all got ruined. He didn't even check if they still worked, just threw them clattering into a big black trash bag and never fished them back out like I would've.

Since then I've read millions of words on pages, millions of first-draft words, millions of published words, written millions of words of my own. But his line of grey plastic games, the way the light slanted in on them through the basement window in the late afternoons when his friends came over after practice to flop on beanbag chairs on the orange shag rug and make fun of each other and play Contra or Excitebike or Mario, the way the labels curled, peeled, and then rubbed off, ruined, after the flood, his childhood's end...strange, the things you never forget.

"Lake of Fire"

The gift store was her first real job, where she filled out tax forms and checked in and out with a time clock. She had started work the day after school got out, and now it was July and she was bored. Eight hours a day shifting from foot to foot on the carpet-covered concrete behind the register, or looking for things to Windex, or organize by color, for old magazines that could be pulled, for greeting cards that were in the wrong section. Eight hours of looking at things that represented the vacation: a coffee mug with shells printed on it, a pencil holder shaped like an Adirondack chair, a cross-stitch kit of a lighthouse. Eight hours of wearing a sweater buttoned up against the cold of the air conditioning.

Every day, when she walked out into summer rising up in the heat from the sun-baked parking lot, when she opened her car door and bent through the rush of warmth to open the window on the passenger side, when she sat on her parents' porch and watched the fireflies lighting on the tangle of wildflowers, darkening with the end of day, and then later when she leaned out her bedroom window with a cigarette, far enough so the smoke wouldn't come back in, and she could hear the peepers and the bigger toads and the running water of the stream out back, she would think that there was more to her than this.

The Fourth of July was the real start of summer – she'd always thought so. The bonfire popping sparks toward the trees, not tinder dry of August or birth wet of June, but the space between, no fear of runaway combustion, no warning. The leaves a dark mass above, latticed like lace, and between them black sky, stars sparkling in and out when the branches swayed in the breeze. The fire cracking, shifting, smoking cinders one way and then another. She looked into the glowing coals, molten, seeing a forge, a cast iron pot, melted silver. Beyond the fire, sand and rocks, and the water lapping the beach. Skin hot on the fireside, cold on the other. Whiskey and cigarettes and openmouthed kisses, bare legs over her boyfriend's lap.

And the next morning, when she woke up on the beach at somebody's parents' cottage on a lake, when she could almost reach the water with her outstretched hand, when she could see the curled metal of sparklers and the torn cardboard of a cherry bomb, when she could see the embers of the campfire dying, she knew she was alive.

The Living

We'd been together a month when she took me out to the suburbs to see her mother's grave. First she drove by the house where she grew up, pointed out where the new people had changed the fence, replaced the picture window with a bay. She looked for so long the car started to veer onto the other side of the street. I felt bad for not warning her before she bumped the curb.

The graveyard was huge and the grass was still green, scattered with red and yellow leaves. I'd never seen graves like that, rows of pink or gray granite with granite vases stuck on top of them. I expected her to lead me to one of those, but instead we went into a building with glass doors like a mall and a room with walls of gravestones piled on top of each other like mailboxes.

"I never feel her here," she said, and I could see why. I couldn't wait to go back out into the bright sunshine, where at least the graves had different flowers in their vases.

On the way home we were mostly quiet until she said, "I'll never love anyone like I loved my mom. She was the love of my life." I rolled down my window then, slowly so as not to make it seem like a comment, and turned my face toward the wind.

Manmade

Five months after she moved in, she found out why the house had been so cheap.

It started with a couple of white pickups with amber lights on top, rambling past on the dirt road. The next week, it was flatbeds with Caterpillars, and then, months later, the white blades covered in shrinkwrap like wintering boats. She watched the procession from her front porch, coffee in hand, as spring turned to summer turned to fall. She didn't like the feeling that she'd been tricked, but didn't mind the construction so much. Sure, it was sad to see the big pines fall, bounce once or twice, lie still with the dust swirling into the air around them. But at least the saws were too far away to be loud. And everyone said that windmills ruined the view, but it meant nothing else would be built on that ridge. They were better than skyscrapers, or Walmarts. So she watched, and rocked in her new painted rocking chair, and drank her coffee, and loved being in this house that was all her own.

For a long time she was alone, but then she met Pete at the coffee shop, and then she started seeing him there every week, and then she started going every morning, when he was most likely to be there. And then one day he said, hey, want to go see the windmills up close?

They drove up in Pete's truck, a red F-150 with the kind of paint that loses its shine after a decade or so. Pete's hands were tanned, rested casually on the steering wheel. They listened to K100, and he talked back to the DJs. The power company had done a good job with the wide, flat road, which was smoother than the town's potholed asphalt.

She saw the first one when they rounded the corner, bigger than she had expected, like a lighthouse. Then when she stepped out of the truck, and the wind hit her full-on, she felt a rush of fear. When she got closer, when she looked straight up at the windmill and it seemed like it was falling toward her, when she saw the shadow of it against the trees behind, when the alien whirr filled her ears like it might never stop, when Pete came to stand beside her, she started to think that maybe none of this had been such a good idea.

Some Other Family

My mother resented going to Canada for every family vacation. It was where my father had gone with his parents, and he loved it, and he was the one who made the money. Mostly we went to Prince Edward Island, with the wide beaches made of soupy clay, the lines of endless gentle breakers, the dune grass. Like my mother, I hated the ocean — all those endless waves going same, same, same, and over, over, over.

My mother sat at the picnic table in the shade, near the swingset, and my father and brothers ran around on the beach like idiots, and when my mother had cleaned up the cookout she'd cooked in the metal grate next to the picnic table, when she had settled back in the beach chair she insisted on carrying with her everywhere (even on the rare occasions when we flew somewhere), and had taken out the latest *National Geographic*, I would go away from her, a few feet at a time, until I was on the edge of the woods, and then until I was just behind the front line of trees that the park's caretaker took care of, and then until I was all the way in the woods, so far in that I couldn't hear the ceaseless sound of waves and wind and gulls and my mother angrily turning the thick pages of her magazine.

So far in that I couldn't have heard her even if she noticed I was gone and called to me. So far in that one time I came out almost to the other side, to some other family's campsite. And I crouched and watched the family, with their pop-up camper and their radio tuned to a baseball game, which I guess had to have been the Blue Jays, or maybe the Expos. Their kids were playing, jumping up and down on a board-and-rope bridge over a little stream. The boy jumped down hard and the girl popped up and laughed, and they did it over and over but the parents never yelled at them to cut it out. And while I was crouching down there, the back of my legs started shaking and I thought about what it would be like to be a major league catcher, crouching down all through a game. But I didn't want to leave. I didn't leave until I could see that the sun was going down, leaving only the tops of the trees still in sunlight. And the last thing I saw before I turned to go was the dad, throwing a baseball up high, so high it could still catch the sun.

Man,
Things Were Getting Good

The night had been work, dinner with friends, a bottle of wine on Fitzie's fire escape. The stack of ones Chuck gave her when she cashed out was too thick for her jeans pocket. She loved the regulars at the restaurant: Matt with the long eyelashes and the moleskine next to his place setting, Carly with rockabilly hair and a green bowling ball bag, Kevin sharing a clove cigarette with her on her fifteen-minute break.

It was the first night that didn't end up too cold for short sleeves. Everything was thick with that early-summer heat, the smell of asphalt and jasmine as they sat on the back steps smoking, and she licked her lips and watched the woods for fireflies.

Dinner was the new guac and basil burger on special, browned just through but juicy. Chuck comped all her friends as a thank you for the double she'd worked a couple days before. She flirted with Jimmy, the new dishwasher, before they left, because it made her feel that everything was hers, everything could be conquered.

They watched *The Last Picture Show* for the hundredth time over at Fitzie's, all of them crowded together on the couch, the smooth skin of their legs and arms brushing against each other, tangling in different combinations over and over. And then after the movie, on the fire escape, she sat with her legs dangling, looking far away to the quiet lights of Center City. They passed the bottle of chianti, hand to hand, mouth to mouth, and she could still taste everything from earlier in the night, the clove and the basil, the butterscotch cannoli she'd sneaked when she first got in. They talked about going down the shore on Friday, about Andrew's band's show at Johnny Brenda's next week. And just before it was time to get on her bike and head home, Dino put his hand on her waist, just for a minute, as he kissed her cheek goodbye. She could smell the spice of his cologne, and she wanted to grab his bicep and squeeze it hard, run her hand down his arm and hook her fingers around his leather belt and pull. But that would be another night. She could wait.

• • •

In the early haze of the next morning, a dog-walker found her. Naked and splayed behind her stepfather's townhouse, bruises all over, she looked like she'd tried to crawl into the bushes at the edge of the parking lot.

Seven days later, the police made their arrest. The kid had confessed after fifteen minutes of questioning. It was random, he said. He saw her bike and wanted it, he said. She fought back.

Pareidolia

In her long days alone in the rented house, she searches for company. Faces of deer in the knotty pine walls, fat ducks in the kitchen canisters, a bent-backed man in the curve of the stairs.

More tangible signs of people come and gone — a filing cabinet stuffed with index cards, worn-out chairs that bear the imprints of bodies, a small handprint low in a kitchen corner.

She sleeps as late as she can each morning, then lies in bed watching the voile curtain move in the breeze. When it rains she breathes in the smell of wet pines and spruces. She waits until the curtain is darkened with drops, then shuts the window and tries to sleep again.

Afternoons she sits in sunlight on the kitchen floor, next to the handprint. She makes herself small again, trying to see the room with a child's complete attention. The way the light moves across the linoleum. The way an ant drags a dead comrade. The bloom of cream in her coffee. If she can keep track of things, if the details matter... maybe.

Swim Team

It was a first day in a flowered beach suit with a back too low. It was a new black Speedo, also with the wrong kind of back. It was two or three torn practice suits on top of each other for extra drag. It was a meet suit so tight you could barely roll it over your hips.

It was crawling in the beginner lane, trailing too close to someone's feet, eye-level with a wart, a flap of skin, a band-aid.

It was anchoring a relay that had been lapped already, swimming alone before a crowd that was done cheering.

It was a hairball in a drain. It was the girl who didn't wear tampons. It was pushing someone's glob of mucus out of your way. It was having a perpetual cold.

It was watching someone flip too close to a wall, hearing the backs of both ankles smack the tile, seeing her body wilt toward the bottom.

It was trying too hard. It was leaving too much for the end. It was counting the laps wrong. It was bruises on your hands from hitting the lane lines. It was terrible chlorinated acned skin.

It was the day the coach turned the lights off and played Aerosmith as the team motorboated back and forth, pushing beat-up kickboards.

It was the smell of your coach when he hugged you as you cried after you lost, how he didn't care if his shirt got wet. It was waiting in the bleachers for your race, listening to mixtapes of Dr. Dre and Snoop Dogg. It was pulling yourself out of the pool at the end of a good swim, how your arms shook.

It was frozen hair and cold car rides. It was a heavy bag full of wet towels, finding space to dry them in your parents' crowded bathroom. It was being bone-tired with homework still to do.

It was leaning down at the end of a lane to cheer on a friend.

It was someone making fun of the Head and Shoulders your mom bought you, because your mom thought shampoo was shampoo. It was everyone seeing your underwear. It was growing your leg hair from fall to spring and wondering whether to shave your arms for States.

It was the bright yellow panic of trying to swim the whole length of the pool underwater. It was getting up on Christmas Eve morning and driving to practice, the heavy doors and the quiet changing room. It was your heart, feeling it beat.

Putting It Back

Her favorite old photographs are the ones with the flashes of light, like this, with the sun shooting off the bus's window. In another, a pregnant woman in a dotted dress holds something she must have moved quickly: cupped in her hands, the light tinders, flares.

The room is small and off the kitchen. For another family, it could have been a mud room, or a walk-in closet, or even plumbed to be an extra bathroom, something useful. She keeps the door closed to company, but when she goes in she opens the curtains to the row of icicles, gleamed and dripping.

She's stacked the pictures in shoeboxes, tied them with twine. On each is a piece of an index card labeled "Luggage" or "Garden Hoses" or "Fur Coats," "Dogs' Collars" or "Adventure Books" or "Fishing Trophies". "Rhinestone Sunglasses," "Crocheted Blankets," "Costume Jewelry".

The night of the fire had been humidity waiting to break, the stream running high, frogs calling from tree to tree. She woke first, to the campfire smell, the smoke rolling low over their beds like fog through the islands. She had dreamed it many times before, many times since, the slow-motion burn, the what-to-take. She didn't take anything.

Separation

1.

The water moves slow, slower, until it's barely going anywhere. It freezes around the edges first, but then those parts shatter, float out with the new water the spring brings in. On one cold night it freezes in the middle, thicker and thicker then up to the shore. It booms at night. It's transparent black, then white, then covered with snow. In the spring it gets rotten, long-crystaled like the ground frost. It breaks and floats. It melts. The water warms. It swells and recedes. The tops of the rocks show, show more. The lilypads break the surface, bloom.

2.

Dive down below the surface, breaking that plate glass calm, reflecting trees and white of sky, overcast. Below, I lean my head back, plug my nose, rise up to where the water meets sky.

3.

Sometimes I miss the way everything unfamiliar looked so clear. The way every brick in the sidewalk stood separate, like everything looks when you get done crying. But also lined with sadness still, like when I got my new glasses back from the eye doctor, and every lampshade had a line of rainbow on the edge, primary colors that expanded if I moved my head just so.

Chromatic aberration, my dad said. We were a crossword family, a *Jeopardy!* family. We were precise. Winter nights my dad and I trudged with flashlights down the rocky path to the lake, crunched across the frozen cove to the spot where the sky was a bowl above us. Dad found Cassiopeia, Ursa Minor, Io and Ganymede and Betelgeuse, his professor voice naming them for me.

4.

In the city park, I lie on my back, trying to make up for miles and miles of my feet touching only pavement. Shades of overarching branches, leaf cover cool, smell of new, not too wet but not dry either, leaves newborn all over, unfurling to open.

Soon,
You Will Have to Worry

The night has chilled enough for sweatshirts, sweaters, fleece jackets, after a long, cloudless afternoon in which you lay on the grass with Sean and Jason and Mike and Josh, arms spread out and fingers almost close enough to touch. Mike grabbed one of your flip flops and wedged it beneath his head for a pillow, and you were glad it was new enough to smell more of Walmart than of bare feet. Looking up at the deep blue sky, you knew how lucky you were.

Now the wind swishes through the pines above the back deck where you are drinking a glass of wine and smoking a clove cigarette so slow that it keeps going out. This afternoon, everyone was still, and you could imagine that they were imagining their bodies sinking into the grass and the dirt, like you were, and when Josh said, "what was that poem where the bodies become part of the ground?", you said "Thanatopsis" without even having to think.

This afternoon you didn't have to think too hard about anything, hold on to anything, but now Mike is doing that thing again, that frenzied thing, and even though you can smell the pines and see the stars overhead when you lean back in your lawn chair, you can also smell the lighter fluid, the hair Mike burned on his arm, you can see the bright flashes of the fire.

Stealing Signs

My boyfriend's parents' Airstream trailer was full of signs he'd stolen. The trailer was parked for good at the end of a narrow dirt road, and his parents never used it anymore. The coffee table said Stop. Frost Heave hung on the bathroom door. He'd stacked orange cones in a kitchen corner, and one morning we woke up to a Railroad Crossing pole stuck six feet out into the pond.

I yelled for an hour when he brought in the purple garden ball on the sandstone stand, and I stomped up and down the trailer's tiny hallway. Stealing from the town was okay, but I didn't like him making off with things from people's yards. I didn't want him to be that person.

On summer weekends he had parties at the trailer. His parents bought the alcohol, delivered it to us, and then left us alone. He was their youngest child by eighteen years.

Later I read in the newspaper that four kids went to jail for stealing a Stop sign because somebody ran through it and got killed. But it's all so arbitrary, you know? What counts as a crime and what doesn't. What can be stopped.

"Through the Never"

I think I heard it. It was like a door slamming upstairs. Sometimes the doors slammed like that when it was windy and the language teachers left their classroom windows open. I was in the school after school, probably in the library like usual.

They found the body that night. This kid Hollis found it, this kid Hollis who had a unibrow that he smoothed over and over with his fingertips when he stood on the diving board about to do a dive. Hollis was on the prom committee. The prom committee was in the auditorium decorating for the prom. Hollis had gone upstairs for something, he went upstairs to find more decorations or something, into the dressing rooms on the sides of the stage that we only used during plays or musicals. He went upstairs and he saw the body, and he told Mr. Harrison, and Mr. Harrison went upstairs and he saw the body too. Later, months later, in our junior English class, Mr. Harrison read us a piece of prose he had written about that night. I don't know what he wanted us to say about it. It was like he wanted us to help him carry it, or something, like he didn't want to be alone with it anymore. He said the body was pale and slumped against the wall. He mentioned the blood. For a long time after that I would imagine the body when I closed my eyes in the shower, imagine it slumped against my parents' bathtub. I imagined it the way Mr. Harrison described it. I never heard how Hollis described it.

The next day when we were posing for prom pictures at Cascade Park, Kristen said Hollis was "pretty shook up". She said it like of course he was, anybody would be. Veronica almost cried but stopped because of her eye makeup, and she said she didn't know how we could enjoy the prom now, after what happened, but she was just saying it to get attention like always. She was lucky to get attention for feeling bad about that kid instead of for her prom dress, which was cut so low that when she went to pick up her blind date, who was a freshman at another school, she made Kristen pretend to be her. The blind date's parents weren't fooled.

Veronica didn't know that kid who died and neither did I. Neither did Hollis. All the kid did was wrestling, and nobody went to wrestling meets. Or matches. Or whatever.

But some kids went to his funeral, and they said the casket was plain wood and people wrote messages on it in Sharpie. They said people put bottles of alcohol in there with him, and joints, and Metallica and Iron Maiden CDs. I wonder what his parents thought about that. I wonder how long it had been since they'd known their son that well.

Wild Like Fire

And sometimes she wants to get out of the car, right after they break out of the city or right before going in. Swing the heavy door out and open, sneaker scuff once and twice on the rumble strip, and then she's on the shoulder, gray sand strewn with broken red taillight. She's down the embankment, tall grass swishing around her legs, legs ahead of her, unbalancing her. The woods ahead, the places the sun reaches and the places it does not. Brittle sticks sticking out, low branches on the trees, she crashes through, she dodges trunks the way she has learned to dodge people on the sidewalk, her eyes low, anticipating. Keeps on beyond the ding of the car door open, beyond the traffic river-roar, footfalls deep in pine needles and black mud that sucks at her shoes.

Once she saw a kid with a lighter, teenage, holding it up to the map of Prospect Park, flame close enough to melt the cover, the smell of plastic burning acrid. She saw him, one hand on the lighter, the other cupping away the wind. She saw how bad he needed that wildness, a dusktime kid outside a park of paved trails, outside bikers and runners steady on the hamster wheel. A park full of city. A park with cast iron gates that locked him out at night.

Sometimes she wants to, but she doesn't. She never does.

Sledding

Remember what it feels like when snow wedges between boot and bare leg? How your skin turns red and you can see your pores and you brush at the snow with your mitten to get it out fast? Some melts. The melted snow gets the top of your sock wet. Your sock is already scrunched down around your heel because of the boot, because of the running around. Your sock's wet and your ankle hurts with cold, but it doesn't hurt enough to go inside.

You pull the leg of your snow pants back around the boot where it belongs and you grab your red plastic sled, last-year's sled, faded from being stored under the deck, just barely in the path of the sun. The sled has some brown leaves frozen into the back of it, in the hollow part behind the seat. You'd think the leaves would have shaken loose when you flipped the sled, but they didn't, not yet.

You run uphill, next to the sled path that's been smoothed by the sleds going down, messed up only a little bit near the bottom where you dumped it last time. You pull your sled behind you by the rope and you dig the toes of your boots into the snow hard to get enough traction to climb the hill. You look back when one of your sled's metal brakes catches. You look back just a little too long and maybe you've veered into the sled path a little bit, a wayward step when your going-forward was stopped by the brake catching.

You look back for just long enough to pull your sled free, and when you look forward, BAM, your brother hits you full-on, his hard head catching your chin, making you fall over backward and wedging your boot full of snow again. Your face hurts from the impact and the cold and your brother's snowsuited body is on top of your snowsuited body and you push him off. Then he pushes you because you pushed him and because you were in the way.

And you never, even for a minute, imagine that you'll miss this someday, that your body will miss the impact of his body, that you'll miss all those times when you fought in the snow and he was right there at arms' length. You lie back and he lies back, and you and he are breathing hard and sweating in your snowsuits, and you're upside down on the hill with the blood rushing into your heads. You look up at the night sky, the tree branches, the dizzying stars.

Starting Over

She looks at his plate. She waits. He's talking about his job again, the job where he works with people she's not close enough to know. *Yet*, she should think, not close enough yet. Maybe someday she will know all his friends. She will go to his sisters' baby showers and cut his grandparents' obituaries from the newspaper.

They will drive somewhere far, late at night, and she will help him stay awake. They will sing along to the radio station and will make up new words for the songs. They will remember those words as if they are the real ones.

He will ask her where something is – the cooler, the screwdriver, the Fix-a-Flat for a punctured tire. And she will know. She will yell directions from a different room.

He will know her favorite kind of Ben and Jerry's. He will pick it up at the store when he gets his favorite. They will sit on the couch with their pints and spoons, and she will make sure her foot is close enough to feel his leg through his jeans.

She will know that he likes to sit through the credits at the end of a movie, or wait until the crowd clears at a baseball game. Someday, some of the things he likes will become things she likes, and she will forget why.

Someday, they will be like saplings winding their branches together. They will be a tongue and a groove. They will be salt and pepper.

Someday, she'll take the pickles off his plate as soon as the food comes, before the pickle juice soaks into the chips. But today she just watches it happen. She watches and waits.

Fish Dreams

1.

The other day I wrote a lie I hate to re-read:

Lie #2: I love eating live fish from fishtanks. I love the way they flip around in my mouth, and the way they go limp when I bite down. I keep the limp body in my mouth for a second before I swallow. It makes me feel powerful.

2.

Sometimes, half-awake in grey morning light, I imagine there are dead goldfish in my bed, near my feet. It's all I can do not to flail away from them. This has happened more than once.

3.

Larger dead fish don't bother me so much.

4.

Begin again. I remember a dead fish on a lakerock. I didn't know what it was at first, and I asked my grandmother to get it for me. I don't remember what happened then. She didn't pick it up or anything. No screaming. It was shiny silver. It was on its side.

Also, the fish in our fishtank, having babies one morning before church, right after Dad got the new car. All the babies swimming around, and then we realized that the mother was eating them. Mom put a glass pitcher over the mother, to keep her from eating her children. But they died anyway. They swam around, big-eyed, until the mother gulped them up.

Now I'll probably have those fish-dreams again.

5.

These days, I don't close my eyes in the shower for long. But I used to sometimes imagine fish floating around my ankles in the backed-up water.

6.

I hate fishtanks, but love aquariums. At the Boston Aquarium I saw a school of silver fish, moving fast, all in the same direction, except for one that was dead. The body was sort of moving in the same direction, but not really keeping up. Its eye was wide and staring, but then all the live ones' eyes were too. I didn't mind that dead fish, but I still remember it.

I can hear the trashtruck picking up the dumpster in the street below our apartment. It picks it up and shakes the dumpster into itself, and there's the sound of glass breaking. I bet it smells like fish. Dead fish. That's what they usually smell like.

I had a scratch-n-sniff sticker that ostensibly smelled like dead fish. I took it with me to my grandfather's funeral. On it was a picture of a trashcan with a limp fish on top, with an x for an eye. The dead Boston Aquarium fish did not have an x for an eye.

7.

In college my next-door neighbor had one leg. He was very good at skiing. Skiing and banging on girls' doors in the middle of the night, demanding to be let in. He was going away on a skiing trip and he had a fishtank and he asked if he could leave the fishtank in my room while he went away on his trip. He promised that he would take me skiing later in the winter if I fishsat for him. Reluctantly, I said okay. I remember him standing next to my dorm room window, after having put his fishtank on the windowsill. He moved slightly awkwardly, but was really barely hampered by only having the one leg. He was pouring water into the tank and I was looking on with dread, and I finally said, "I can't do it. I hate fish." It was awkward, but I knew I couldn't handle it, a weekend with fish in my room.

8.

Begin again. I also don't mind when the lake fish bite my toes. It's startling, but okay. I kick at them, and they go away. They have hard mouth ridges, not differentiated teeth. At least, that's what it feels like. I assume that to be true.

I assume a lot of things to be true that may not actually be true. Perhaps that's one of my faults. Or strengths.

9.

I have a bag of frozen shrimp in the freezer. We have eaten almost everything in the apartment, in preparation for moving. But the bag of shrimp is still there. It's been there for a long time, because the last time I thawed some of those shrimp bodies and ate them I realized how similar to fish bodies they were. "Come on," L said, "don't do that to yourself. You love shrimps." I do. But the fact remains, they are little dead fish bodies. Not quite as slippery as goldfish, at least. I think it would actually be better if they were the peel-and-eat kind, with legs on. Peeling them would distract me, I think. Now, that is odd. Why do I make these distinctions?

10.

This all makes me sound like I am obsessed with fish. But really I only think about them once in a while. They're on my mind because I just read a passage in a book about a girl's fish dying when someone unplugged their tank overnight. The girl and her father flushed the fish down the toilet. That is not what we did in our family. Our plumbing was too unreliable, so we buried our fish in margarine containers.

11.
What is the opposite of dead fish? Iowa? Yes, that. Somewhere as far away from water as possible. Wide plains-n-prairies. Buffalo with their shaggy dusty coats and formidable horns.

Packing boxes half-full of not-fish. Eyes heavy-lidded, mind clear of fish, mind full of tumbleweeds that bounce along a dusty, deserted street, leaving no trails.

House of Tea

The three of you have just turned off South Street toward Fabric Row, and already the city seems calmer, the streets lined with more trees. Nancy wants to stop in the House of Tea, so the three of you go in. You've been thinking about becoming a tea drinker. Your parents drink tea, cup after cup all day long. When you were a kid you had the whole collection of china animals that came in the boxes of Red Rose, some in doubles and triples.

The store has two rooms with painted wood floors. You and Allison go into the room that has the tea sets and diffusers and cups with lids. The Burmese restaurant had teacups with lids, and now you are on a mission to get some, too. When Nancy took the lid off her cup at the Burmese restaurant, it slid along the table and almost fell off. You would never put the tea lid on the table with the underside down, because you would know it would be wet with condensation, and you wouldn't want to leave a wet ring on the table. But Nancy doesn't think about things like that. The tea in the Burmese restaurant is jasmine tea that smells better than it tastes.

Your mother used to say, "I'll make some tea to bring Dad home." When you and your mother and brother walked in the door late after gymnastics classes in town, your dad would say, "I just put the tea on."

You and Allison go into the main room, where there is a wooden bar at chest height. Black tins line the walls. There are eight shelves with twenty tins on each. Each tin has a gold emblem on the front that says "House of Tea".

You used to be in a writing group that met at the house of a person named Zephyr. Zephyr made tea with flavors like anise or blackberry, and he served it in hand-thrown mugs with no handles. This is partly why you want to get into tea, because you remember Zephyr measuring the tea into the infuser, how evenly he poured it into the cups.

Nancy is asking the shopkeeper what's in the Noel blend. Nancy is into tea shops, not necessarily into drinking tea. You've had tea at her house before, watery Earl Grey. Her apartment is full of thin flowered teacups with saucers, some of which she inherited from her grandmother. She has started a collection of tea towel souvenirs from the places she's visited. She is considering a part-time job working at a tea shop on weekends, not because she needs the money but because she wants to meet people. You hate to think about how lonely your two best friends are. You hate to think about them coming home to empty apartments, the long Saturdays and Sundays waiting to be filled with errands and naps.

"It's too complex to explain," the shopkeeper tells Nancy, about the Noel blend. "You'll just have to smell it."

The shopkeeper is a very small woman, and later you will wonder how she managed to get the tea tins down from the highest shelves. You don't remember seeing her struggle to reach them. Nancy smells the Noel blend. You and Allison smell it too. It doesn't smell like cinnamon, like you expected. It smells like dried orange peels and maybe cloves, and maybe peppermint, but not too much. It *is* complex, and it is dark and mysterious and sort of ghostly, things you love about Christmas but can't put exactly into words. It smells like that Wyeth painting *Christmas Morning*, with the snow melting around the old man's body. But not the body, of course, just the feeling of Christmas ghosts, Christmases that have gone and gone and gone before.

Nancy nods at the woman and doesn't say anything after she smells it. You and Allison thank the woman and keep looking up at all those tins of tea.

You say, "I'm a coffee drinker, but I'm thinking about getting into tea. Do you recommend anything?"

"Do you like the taste of coffee, or just the caffeine buzz?" the woman says. Her light blue eyes are spaced wide apart.

"I like the taste. I also like Chinese tea, and my boyfriend drinks green tea."

"Well, the Chinese tea is a different end of the spectrum. If you like the taste of coffee you'll like the black teas." The woman pulls down canisters for you to smell. Allison smells them too.

"If you like the way tea smells, you'll like the taste," the woman says.

You like the way all of them smell. You wonder where Nancy is.

"My parents drink tea all day," you say. "My dad's British."

The woman nods. "I drink tea as soon as I get up in the morning," she says. "I make it in a pot on the stove. Never drink coffee, don't like the taste."

"I like jasmine tea, too," you say.

"I have a great jasmine tea. It's the only one I sell in two ounce packages."

You smell the jasmine tea. It smells great. "I'll take some of that," you say. "How do you recommend I make it?"

"You don't want to bother with any of these infusers. Just put the tea leaves right in the bottom of the cup. You only need three of the jasmine leaves. Let it brew for two minutes, then take the leaves out with a spoon. You can reuse the leaves twice, maybe three times if you have a good palate."

It goes on. The woman talks about the merits of tea vs. coffee (coffee beans are ground, while tea leaves stay whole. The whole leaves impart a purer, more consistent flavor), about the steady caffeine distribution tea gives, about the nutrients green tea provides. Then she tells you that she is a jockey, that she inherited the tea shop when her father died, that she ran ten miles that morning.

Nancy is sitting in an armchair behind you, writing in her notebook. This is a bad sign. You've only known Nancy to write in a notebook when she's copying down a recipe at Allison's house or when she's mad. But you can't think why she's mad.

You buy four ounces of tea called After Snow Sprout, because you love the name. The three of you go out into the sunny day. Nancy isn't speaking. You can't figure it out, and don't until much later.

It's an extension of a long-running hurt. The tea lady spoke to you, and not to her. You have a partner, you have a job you like. When you make tea, somebody will come home.

A Clean Break

The sun was in my eyes, but that's not why it happened. Really I could see pretty good. Not perfect, but I'd driven with the sun in my eyes before. The morning fog was still there, low in the fields. I'd left Lila's house about six and drove her long dirt driveway to the main road. The blueberry barrens were that dark red, the color they get at the tail end of the season.

Lila had made me some strong coffee. I held my plastic travel mug between my legs as I drove. I thought about the day ahead and the energy seemed like it went right out of my arms and legs. Gramp told me once that when my uncle Bub died it took the starch out of him for a long time. That's the way I'd felt all fall.

I was thinking about Lila as I drove. I'd been spending most nights at her house this fall. We didn't sleep in the same room, of course. I'd become a true Christian only recently, but I knew the Bible was very clear on some things. It sounds crazy, but I didn't mind not sleeping together. Her parents' house had a finished basement. I had a lot of my stuff over there, so it felt like home, better, in some ways. My mom had just moved again, to an even smaller place, so if I wanted to stay over there I slept on the couch. My dad's house is nice and big, but it's an even longer drive from there to the base.

When I turned onto Route 1 I saw a big buck and a couple of does, across the field near the causeway. I thought about calling my dad on the cell phone. Looked like a real nice buck, and he didn't have his yet. But he wouldn't get there in time. The fields are full of deer on days when you can't go hunting, but they disappear real fast when you've got a gun in your hand.

I was getting sick of driving back and forth to the base. It was a three-hour round trip, and I did it every day. There were so many better things to do with the time I had left. Spend time with my little nephew, maybe, or go hunting with Dad. Maybe I wouldn't get to go hunting again. And I hated to think how much Alex would grow up while I was gone. My sister had taught him some sign language, so he already knew a lot of words – seemed like every day he picked up a few more. Joanne got him this teddy bear and had me record myself talking. When Alex grabs the bear's paw, he can hear me saying hello. Kid's gonna be confused if he ever sees me again. When, I guess I should say.

Lila had cooked me a big breakfast that morning, like she did every morning before I went to the base. I wished she wouldn't. I don't like eggs much, and I'm not big on bacon either. I'd be happy enough with one of those breakfast bars on the way out the door. But she insisted. Said I needed my nutrients. I knew she was worried about a lot more than me not getting enough to eat, so I let her fuss. I didn't pay much attention to her anymore, to be honest. Just let her do her thing. I'd tried to break up with her more than once. Seemed unfair to make her wait for me, when I'd be gone at least eighteen months. But every time I tried to sit down and talk about it, something kept me from saying what I needed to.

I was wearing my sweatshirt, but it was cold that day and I should've had on my jacket too. It was lying next to me on the seat of the truck, I remember that. I also remember thinking that it would be strange not to wear my own clothes much anymore. Not that I cared about clothes at all, but still. It seemed strange. Every day I thought of more things I'd be giving up and more ways my life was going to change. I remember I was holding onto the steering wheel pretty tight, thinking bout Lila. She was a good girl, and she just loved the hell out of me. That's why I hadn't been able to break up with her, and why I thought I should.

The week before, just after we got the call, I went over to her house. I sat down at the kitchen table with her mother first, because I wanted to make everything clear. But when I tried to explain, it came out all wrong. I couldn't make her understand why we had to break up. I remember exactly what it was like in the room that night, how the kitchen was scrubbed so clean the countertop sort of reflected the light over the sink. I could smell dish detergent and hear *Wheel of Fortune* on in the other room.

Lila's mom just looked at me for a little while, and then she said, "Do you love her?"

It was like she was looking right into my brain with those light blue eyes, the same ones Lila had. And I knew that Lila's mom was smarter than me. Closer to God, too. My relationship with Him was just starting – I couldn't read His signs too well yet. Like I said before, I didn't know the Bible too well either, but I was reading it. It was slow going, but I started at page one and kept at it. So Sharon looked at me and asked me that, and I wasn't going to lie to her. But the truth was that love didn't have anything to do with this particular situation.

"Yes," I said to Sharon, "I do love her. That's why I don't want her wasting her senior year waiting around for me." I thought that was about as honest as possible, so it shocked the hell out of me when Sharon went over to the silverware drawer and came back with a jewelry box. In it was a diamond ring, just the plain gold band and the big stone like everyone seems to want. She'd been saving it for when I was ready, she said. It was Lila's grandmother's ring.

"You know Lila's crazy about you," Sharon said. "It scares me to think what she'd do if you broke up with her. Put your trust in Jesus, who guides us." She handed me the box. By now I had that ache around my eyes, the dull pain I'd been feeling a lot lately. Maybe my body knew what was going to happen, I don't know.

Sharon and I talked for a while longer, but nothing we said mattered much. Then Lila's dad came in and I asked if I could ask. Finally I went in to the living room and gave the ring to Lila. And she was so happy, happier than I'd seen her since I got the call, and it almost made it seem right. And I really did love her.

I don't mean to make excuses, but by then I was just real tired. It didn't seem to make much difference whether I broke up with Lila or not. Either way, she was going to be unhappy when I left. Either way, I was going into some crazy dust storm of a country, and I knew I probably wasn't coming back. I'd had a dream a few nights before.

We were sitting down in the mess hall, some kind of tent actually, all of us guys from my unit. We were sitting there, having dinner, and then the wall blew out. And everyone around me was dead. It wasn't like one of those cartoon dreams, where you know someone's dead but they don't look it. I don't want to say any more about it, but this wasn't that kind of dream. I don't know if this was a sign from Him or what, but if so it wasn't a good one.

So Lila's family put an engagement announcement in the paper, and they announced it at church. Lila's family had always been real good to me, so I was glad to make them happy. My family wasn't too happy, though. None of them cared much for Lila. I'd seen them make fun of her lisp and the way she walked with her chest stuck out like a little banty rooster. They thought I didn't notice them making fun of her, but I did. And I knew that Lila wasn't a real pretty girl, but she had a good heart. I liked the way she walked, actually. It made me feel like protecting her.

My mom's side of the family just didn't like that I spent more time with her parents than with them, but the truth was I was more comfortable with Lila's family. They understood my commitment to Jesus. They didn't think it was a phase I was in, which is what my mom thought. My mom didn't want to hear me talk about religion. She thought I only cared about Jesus because of Lila and that wasn't true at all.

That morning, in the truck, I turned a corner and I was driving into the sun again. I thought of Lila flashing her ring around, how it caught the light. I thought about holding her hand and how I could feel the ring between our fingers. She must have showed that ring to everyone we knew.

Hanging from my truck's rearview mirror was this carved wooden fish ornament that my older brother's girlfriend gave me for Christmas. I got to thinking about my brother. I remembered how he warned me not to get involved with the military, how he explained why we might end up going to war. It sounded so far-fetched at the time that I didn't pay much attention. That was before I met Lila. I just wanted a change. I was sick of how everyone in my family was always digging around in everyone's business. Like they didn't have anything better to do.

The army sounded like a pretty good deal. Some of my cousins had done it, and now they had good jobs and nice houses. I'd stay in the reserves for a few years and get some money saved up. I had this plan to buy some land and put my mom's old camper on it. Then I'd live in that until I had enough money to build my house. I wanted to teach at the high school and coach track someday. I figured the military could get me my college money.

So, just after graduation, class of 2002, I went to boot camp and did pretty well there. The physical stuff was nothing compared to track season, and I can keep my mouth shut and take orders. But I missed home so bad. I hated being away for those six weeks, and I never wanted to leave again. When I came home from boot camp, it was such a happy time. That's when my sister had Alex and I started dating Lila.

A year and a half later, when my unit got the call, my brother got on the internet and looked up ways to break someone's leg without messing it up permanently.

"Just a clean break," he said to me. "It won't hurt too bad." My brother is smarter than I'll ever be. He's smarter than anyone I know. He doesn't believe in God, though. My ultimate goal is to educate him about that. It would be great to be able to teach him something.

So I was thinking about my brother that morning, and my sister and her little boy. I was thinking about how Lila would be a real good mother, and about how bad I wanted kids of my own. I glanced over at the woods on the side of the road, then I flipped my sun visor up. I let go of the steering wheel, closed my eyes, and prayed for a clean break.

The Wild West

Aunt Mary lives in a condo with white walls. The paint in the bathroom looks just like the paint in the guest bedroom, kind of textured, but it doesn't feel the same. The paint in the bathroom feels like plastic and the paint in the bedroom feels like chalk.

When I think about who Aunt Mary was on her wedding day, it makes me sad. She keeps her wedding album on the shelf in her current living room, and on the first night of my visit, we look through the pictures. Aunt Mary was strikingly beautiful, with her slightly crooked smile and her Jackie O wedding dress with the three-quarter length sleeves.

Aunt Mary isn't technically my aunt anymore, because my uncle divorced her twenty years ago. He left her because he freaked out about his father dying, the story goes, but also because she had gained all that weight after having their two sons. When I think of how I knew Aunt Mary when she was still officially my aunt, I remember her in a black, skirted swimsuit in their pool in Long Island, carefully keeping her hair out of the water and chatting with my mother about raising kids.

It seems to me that Aunt Mary was happier in Long Island than she is here, although she tells me, several times over the course of my visit, that she is happy now. She points out the convenience of her condo's location: five minutes away from Starbucks, Chipotle, Jamba Juice, Rumbi, Borders. Five minutes away, it turns out, from a bus that will take us into Denver, something that Aunt Mary has not yet done in the five years she's lived here.

We go to the city, and once we are there, we're not quite sure what to do. We go into Office Depot to look at that scanner I told Aunt Mary about, the one that scans old slide photographs. That takes ten minutes. Aunt Mary suggests Jimmy John's for lunch, but I don't want to eat anything I could get in my own city. But I don't tell her this. Instead, I suggest bagel sandwiches from Einstein's. Aunt Mary recounts the story of her grandson, who pointed out that Albert Einstein was a scientist, but now he just makes really good food.

After a lunch during which an old man asks me to watch his things while he uses the restroom: his newspapers and books and a fur coat elaborately draped over the table, Aunt Mary and I walk out into the aggressive sunlight of 16th Street. I keep reminding myself to drink from my big bottle of water. I hear the Rockies have to keep their baseballs in a special humidor to keep them from shriveling up to less than regulation size. I imagine myself similarly shriveling.

My head aches, and I don't know if it's the altitude. We get on the 16th Street shuttle and ride it all the way to the capital building. I'd like to climb the steps, to reach the 13th step, where I will officially be one mile high. But Aunt Mary is not a step climber.

We walk by the library and the Colorado Museum. I suggest that we might want to visit the museum. Mary is incredulous. "That's all Colorado history. You're not interested in that." I am, but for some reason I don't say so. What I really want is to go to the art museum, but Aunt Mary has already said that she's not interested in paying to go there. Still, I look the museum's number up in the guidebook and call, although the building itself is only a hundred feet away from where we sit. The art museum isn't too expensive. I feel bad for pushing it, but I tactfully do, and Aunt Mary agrees that the admission price isn't too bad. She gets a deal for being a Colorado resident and a senior citizen.

We pay and lock our bags in a locker. We have to get back into the locker three times to get things that Aunt Mary has forgotten she needs. Then we wait for the elevator to make three trips without us, packed, as it is, with kids from a field trip.

We go up to the seventh floor, Western Art. Aunt Mary walks quickly through the first room.

"I wish I had one ounce of talent," she says, stopping in front of a Norman Rockwell cover for the *Saturday Evening Post*. I don't know what to say in response to things like this, so I say nothing.

Aunt Mary's feet are hurting her. She tells me to walk around on my own. I feel guilty, but I am also starting to feel that feeling that made me want to come in here in the first place, that feeling that I am not like everybody else, but I am like some people. I want to be kind to Aunt Mary, show her how grateful I am that she's letting me visit and stay in her condo, where I have the whole finished basement to myself. The basement is much larger than the apartment I share with my boyfriend. I want to do everything right with Aunt Mary, so I will have no regrets. But Aunt Mary is telling me to go ahead. She has untied her sneakers and leaned back in a comfortable chair. This museum is full of comfortable chairs; that's part of its immense charm.

I go ahead, thinking I will only go off on my own for a few minutes, and then I will go back to spend time with Aunt Mary. I can already feel the lightness, though, the way it feels to dive into a pool with your clothes on, and then take them off underwater, letting them fall away.

Bike People

We have a new trio of neighbors, two girls and one guy. The guy wears a white fedora and skinny jeans and an Army jacket with tabs on the shoulders. The girls are a matched set, one blond and one black-haired, both small. All three have bikes. The bikes are not mountain bikes. Nothing about these people is rugged. They are so skinny that their skinny jeans are baggy, and they ride bikes that are pastel-colored ten-speeds, crappy city bikes that won't attract the attention of thieves, but will attract the attention of other skinny bike riders, who will admire the bikes' paint jobs. When the Bike People first moved in across the hall, they parked the bikes right in front of the door of our building, in a passageway that is narrow to begin with. Jake wrote a note and put it on the front door:

> *Dear Bike People, Sorry we haven't met yet. Please find somewhere else to park your bikes. They're blocking the door.*

They did move the bikes, but then the bikes blocked the steps to the laundry room, which is in a separate building. One day I was down there doing laundry and I held the door for Tanya, who lives below the Bike People. Tanya was struggling down the steps with her own bike, which is also a ten speed but red with a basket on the front. Tanya asked if I wrote the note, and I hesitated and then said that Jake did. She said she'd write the next one, about the Bike People parking in front of the laundry room, about how maybe they should keep the bikes in their apartment. The point of all this is that we knew the Bike People didn't have a great sense about the needs of other people. We knew that from the beginning.

In the first couple of weeks I often spied on them through the peephole in our door. They live right across the hall from us. The previous tenant was a single man who owned a house at the shore and often left the city. We never heard him and almost never saw him. I wish the Bike People were the same way. The salt-and-pepper girls seem to work together – I see them leaving the apartment at the same time, in some approximation of business clothing. They have an affection for the '80s, these girls, and often incorporate these elements in their style of dress. Pearls, bunchy sweaters, shoulder pads. When the '90s are fully back in, they will adopt those styles. I think it's possible that they were born in 1988. They seem to be upper-level college students, possibly people with internships. During one of their loud parties, I heard Salt yelling that she was now 21, and could therefore buy the beer. I don't know if Pepper is the same age, but I assume so. Salt is friendlier than Pepper, in that she is willing to say hello when I meet her in the alley, and when I say it first. Pepper is not willing to say anything at all.

The first time I talked to Pepper was in that first week, when they were inexplicably keeping their door open all the time. I think it was some sort of holdover from living in a dorm, the expectation that someone would stop by and invite them somewhere. I don't consider myself an unfriendly person, but I really have no interest in socializing with neighbors. They're too close – there's no hiding from them. Better to cultivate a distant but not antagonistic relationship.

Anyway, their door was open, and I was locking our apartment so I could go to work.

"Excuse me," Salt said.

I turned to look at them. They were silhouetted, light coming in from a big window behind. I don't know where Fedora was – it's possible that he has a regular job with regular hours, unlike myself or Salt and Pepper.

"Do you have any bugs?" said Salt.

"Bugs? No."

"Oh. Because we just saw this huge bug in here, so I wondered if you had ever seen one."

"No, I haven't. Knock on wood." I had already gone down two of the stairs. I knocked on the wood banister. Salt and Pepper didn't take this opportunity to introduce themselves, and neither did I.

I was a little scared of them, I have to admit. Groups of girls make me nervous, and Salt and Pepper gave the impression of always having a group around them, even when they were alone. And their clothes — when someone dresses outlandishly, in clothes that are not designed for comfort or for warmth but instead for style, it makes me feel that they are always judging my clothes for their practicality and warmth. I suppose I am afraid that they're judging me like I constantly judge them, and really who cares what they wear? I just wish they were quieter. I wish they and their friends were capable of speaking in a voice below a shout, but that seems to not be the case.

Sometimes I imagine Salt and Pepper's friends coming over the roof that divides our roof decks. I imagine them coming over when Jake and I aren't home, coming in through the unlocked upstairs door. I imagine what it would be like to come home to a full party raging in both apartments, my home suddenly fluid. People taking my books, reading them, tossing them aside somewhere. Our food going over to Salt and Pepper's apartment, never to return. It casts doubt on everything, makes it all seem less secure. It makes me want to move all our important belongings to a storage unit, making our apartment less like home but safer.

As I write this now, I am once again trying to get up the gumption to take my laundry downstairs to the laundry room. I don't want Salt or Pepper or any of their friends to see me doing laundry. It's only three short flights of stairs and two doorways to get to the laundry machines, but I dread it. I don't want to see Salt or Pepper or the friends, or the guy. I am ready to have my own house with my own washing machine and my own dryer. We had those things before we moved to the city, and I hated doing laundry then, too. But I should have appreciated it more. I know this now. It is amazing to have a laundry machine in your own house. To not have to hoard your quarters. To not put off laundry because it's raining. To not have strangers moving your wet underwear from a washer to the top of a dryer because you were ten minutes late getting back.

I am glad that there are still places in the world in which next-door neighbors are not a necessary evil. I imagine living in a place like this: a little house surrounded by trees. In October the trees would drop their leaves and the bare branches would frame a harvest moon, and smoke would rise from our chimney. I would stand outside with my arms wrapped around myself, wearing some kind of large not-stylish-but-warm sweater, and I would look at the moon and be glad that I couldn't see the lights from anyone else's houses. And maybe I would think of Salt and Pepper, but not often, and when I did I would be glad that I was no longer able to hear Salt and Pepper and Fedora and their friends and their TV turned up loud and their shrieks to each other across the apartment. I would be glad not to hear the strange high laugh of one of the girls, a laugh that lingers like the smoke from their long, thin cigarettes, permeating everything.

William Tell

————

Tell me, William, was it worth it? Do you remember the long shadows in that square, the way your shoes scuffed on the cobblestones, the way the multitudes cowered at the perceived authority of one man? Not you. You walked on by. So many of us work and work to make a legacy, but when push came to shove, doing nothing was your spark.

Of course, you had worked. Hours and hours in the woods with your bow had made you an expert in things of this nature. In shadows and light, with live prey and imagined, these skills were your greatest power. Your punishment tested what you did best.

And so you went to another square, another day, this time bound with your son in tow. Your son was scared, of course he was. You worried he wouldn't keep still. At the dinner table, in church, and with his own bow raised, he never kept still. This was a test of his bravery, maturity, as much as your confidence.

The crowd assembled, the same men and women in somber colors that had bowed not to the emperor, but to a symbol only, his raised hat. Did you wish at this point that you had just gone along with them, knowing it was foolish but doing it anyway? Did you see the way the sun shone on your boy's hair and regret your stubbornness? Or did you relish this chance to show your skill, to bite your thumb, as they used to say, at the powers that were?

The crowd went quiet, and you relied on them, too, not to distract you. Everything had to be just right, this golden moment: Boy, arrow, apple, string. Did you pause as you sized up the target? Were you proud of your boy for standing so perfectly still, still like the alpine air on that cool autumn day?

Yes. You pulled the string back, you took aim at the apple, just above the spot where your son shone brightest. You took aim, you let go.

The look on your boy's face when it was over, when he stood flecked simply with apple juice and not with blood. The pride you felt in him, in yourself. The way the crowd cheered.

Later Gessler shook your hand, and it seemed he had decided to make an ally of you. But you remembered those little indignities, the new things the teachers were told to teach, the unfamiliar lessons your son had come home repeating. The new colors on the castle walls and the new taxes at the farmers' market. They called Gessler a military man, but his hand was small and he shook softly. He smiled and asked about the second arrow in your quiver.

If he had been a sporting man, a working man, he would have known. Nobody relies on one arrow alone. Nobody gives himself only one chance. You looked at your son, gave him the old family signal, a nod of the head and he made himself scarce.

"If I'd killed my son, so help me God," you said, still grasping Gessler's hand, "The other arrow was for you."

Cities

In the mornings, the light came in through the green leaves pressing into the open window. The room belonged to his friend, a dancer on tour, it was down the street from the conference hotel.

At night they would go out drinking. At the bar he would get her water when he thought she'd had too much wine. They would sit at outdoor tables and smell the trees cooling down and she would look at the string of lanterns and she could blur them a little with her eyes, and what she wanted was that blurry beauty.

She didn't think much about going home, to the city of sharp edges, the city where she already knew who she was. The city where she knew she didn't fit. She fit in this city, his city, with his friends, who talked quietly at outdoor tables, not loudly like the brash, hard girls in her city. Here they talked slow, their thoughts strung together one after another, bright beads in the candlelight, the lanternlight, the winelight.

They went back to the dancer's room, arm in arm, and he read poetry, and she was too drunk to differentiate the words but not too drunk to know that he was reading to her. Not too drunk to know that she would one day tell her friends about this, this man who was beyond belief, a composite of all the romantic heroes he had read and she had read in books, blended together in Neruda and wine.

In the mornings the sun came through the leaves, the room was leaflit, and she didn't feel fuzzy from the night before, and that was because of the water he made her drink, because he loved her, because he wanted to take care of her, because he wanted to own her, because he wanted her to be his child, because he had once taken care of his mother, because he missed his mother, because he missed being a child. Because he wanted a child. Because he wanted her to be the mother of his children.

She woke up feeling fine, feeling more awake than she did in her city, the city of sharp angles. They went to coffeeshops, they went to bookstores. One bookstore had wooden furniture that looked like it was carved straight out of trees and then smoothed by a thousand hands.

Just outside his city was a waterfall. The waterfall was loud like the fountain in her city. It sounded like the fountain, water slapping hard on hot rocks, hissing into mist. The fountain was the best thing in her city, but it wasn't this. They sat on the bank and watched it, clothes getting damp from mist, and then they walked back over tree roots.

They looked at each other in the gloom of forests, saw the way the shadows fell across each other's faces. The forests reminded her of her real home, they made him seem like home.

She cried at the airport when they parted. It seemed necessary to cry, it seemed natural. On the plane she fell asleep, and when she woke up she was halfway back. When she got to her city, her airport, her husband, you look good he said. You look happy. She was happy. She was happy to see him. She wasn't happy to see the city, though, the hard-edged city.

It took walks at night, slipping through the heavy air, the heavy humid air, the smell of trash and sewers, it took walks by the river, walks by the fountain that sounded the same as the waterfall. It took the cool bookstores, the high-branched city trees, the wind through their branches. It took TV and train rides and her husband there beside her in the dark, his breath even, his sleep easy. It took August, September. It took trips to their first home, their real home, where she could smell the trees cooling at night. It took trips home and trips back to the city. It took late afternoons on the balcony, watching the light slip like butter down the buildings. It took dark movie theaters. It took the smell of warm popcorn, it took baseball games, it took music twisting and weaving through the long days.

By November, when he came to her city to see her, it meant nothing. He meant nothing outside of his city, outside of that leaflit room. He was a character from a book. She had cut him out, paper doll. Cut from her life, thrown away. And with him went the dancer's room, the winelight, his lips around Neruda's lines. With him went the feeling in her fingers. With him went layers of herself, her past, all cut out like paper dolls, blown, with him, to the winds.

Punctuation

Part One: Common Problems

Cody was seventeen.
Cody was in love.
Cody's curfew was midnight.
Cody's girlfriend had freckles.
She had a freckle on her right hip.
Cody circled it in pen.
Cody wrote "Cody's" above the freckle.

Cody left the party, and he died.

The SUV broke the thin skim of ice over the gravel pit and sank to the bottom.

Cody's girlfriend told him not to leave the party, and he didn't want to, but went anyway.
Cody's mom didn't want him to drive fast, but didn't want him to be late, so he drove fast.

Seeing the hole in the ice the next morning, Sgt. Benjamin feared the worst.

The dispatcher who answered Sgt. Benjamin's call knew Cody's family.
Everyone in town knew Cody's family.
Everyone in town knew everyone else in town.

Cody's parents, who had only one child, had been up all night.

Cody, their baby, was below 100 feet of water.
Water, black gravel pit water, surrounded the SUV.
Sarah, Cody's girlfriend, didn't know yet.
Marcia and Phil, Cody's parents, didn't think to tell her.

Cody had, a few years ago, stopped telling his parents everything.
Cody knew, or thought he knew, he was going to die.

He dreamed he was in a car accident (driving his father's car, not his mom's SUV) and the dream ended in darkness.

Cody told his girlfriend – he told her everything – and she made him stop talking about it.

She put his finger on her freckle, his favorite one, and made his finger trace back and forth across her stomach until he wasn't thinking about the dream anymore.

Who would open his Christmas presents, he thought, if he died? Would they just stay, with big homemade bows on top, in his parents' bedroom closet?

(That made Cody cry sometimes, as he lay in bed, thinking of the Christmas presents getting dusty, the boxes warping from summer heat, the paper fading.)

The gravel pit was deep, the weather was cold, and visibility was poor.
Cody's mother wanted the police to send divers, a crane, and a submarine, if that's what it would take to get to her son (she couldn't say the word "body").

Part Two: End Punctuation

Marcia was amazed that people could continue on as normal.
She felt skinless.
The police wanted to wait until spring to recover the car.

Marcia asked them how they could leave a kid underwater all winter.

Marcia had always avoided confrontation. But not now.

Sgt. Benjamin said, "I'm sorry, Marcia. I can't endanger my men." She would have gladly traded all of his living men for her dead child.

"The divers can't do their jobs?" Marcia said, "Is that it? Or maybe you don't think the car's really there?"
Sgt. Benjamin said, "It broke through the guardrail, remember? We know it's there. Why don't you sit down?"
"You have children!" Marcia yelled. "I know you understand!"

Part Three: Making Transitions

The other Sarah, Sarah Bunker, was the one who told Cody's girlfriend Sarah; Sarah Bunker's father was a volunteer firefighter.

Sarah and the other Sarah weren't friends; still, the other Sarah thought Cody's girlfriend should know before everyone else.

Sarah skipped the assembly and left the school building; in the meantime, Sgt. Benjamin was on the phone with the Environmental Protection Agency, at Marcia's request.

Here's what Sarah saw as she walked: icy trees, shining in the sunlight; a pink knitted mitten, frozen into a snowbank; a pothole, layered with thin ice.

Sarah jumped on the pothole until it was filled with nothing but snow. She kept walking, even though it was five below and she didn't have her jacket; she didn't stop until she got to the 7-11 where her mother worked.

Sarah's mother stood behind the cash register, selling Steve a breakfast sandwich; Sarah waited in line to talk to her.

Sarah told her mother what she knew: that Cody was dead, that she had left school, and that she needed permission to get a tattoo.

Sarah's mother had plenty of questions: What happened to Cody? Would her daughter be all right? Why a tattoo? For God's sake, a tattoo? Now?

While Sarah's mother hesitated, Sarah blinked back tears and stared at the sign by the register: "Leave a penny, take a penny."

Sarah's mother looked at the clock: 8:45. A woman she didn't recognize stood behind Sarah holding a booklet, "We, Like Sheep: Bible Verses for Every Occasion." While she thought about the tattoo request, Sarah's mother rang up the woman's purchase. Looking for a sign, she opened to a random passage: Luke 1:34. "'How will this be,' Mary asked the angel, 'since I am a virgin?'" This didn't help.

"Mom," Sarah said, almost whispering, "It's going to wear off."

She turned down the waistband of her jeans, and her mother saw the word written above her daughter's right hip: Cody's.

At the crash site, Marcia hadn't given up.

Now Charlie O'Hallahan, the local diver, was talking to Sgt. Benjamin: "Guess if I can dive for urchins in the winter, I can't refuse on account of the cold. I d'no but it'll be tough, though, Benny, gettin' that car door open."

"Just try," Marcia said. "I won't leave him there; don't ask me to."

Part Four: Possessives

Cody's family's house was already lit up for Christmas. In two weeks' time, Marcia's sister Pam and Cody's cousins, Chuck and Casey, would be there for Christmas Eve.

Marcia sat in her husband's car after he had gone inside. She looked at the sign next to the mailbox: "The Joneses' Abode." Her husband's best man gave it to them as a wedding present 25 years ago. He thought it was funny: keeping up with the Joneses, ha, ha. Phil and Cody had wrapped lights around the signpost in a candy cane pattern. The lights were off, but covered in ice and catching sunlight.

They'd been on a fool's errand. She sat up straighter.

"It's a mistake," she yelled, hitting the cold steering wheel. Her hand stung. "It's just a mistake. Cody, I thought you were dead!"

Phil came back out, opened her door and reached for her. "It's time to come inside," he said. "It's been a long morning."

Part Five: Emphasis

Phil felt punch-drunk. Three days ago, he had returned from a fact-finding business trip. His company had taken care of him: he had flown first-class and enjoyed a few well-earned in-flight drinks. But he had felt unsettled. While he waited in the baggage-claim area, he had a feeling that something was wrong at home. Cody had been testing the limits lately, pushing for more independence. Phil had often felt like the go-between in conflicts with his wife and son. He called home. Everything was fine there.

Still, the strange feeling remained. Phil stopped in one of the airport stores. He looked at the quarter-, half-, and one-pound bags of dark chocolate. Cody loved dark chocolate. It had been a while since Phil had bought him a present on a business trip.

Now Phil went into his son's room. The one-pound bag of chocolate sat on Cody's desk, half empty. Phil hesitated, then reached into it. He put a dark wafer of chocolate on his tongue and let it melt.

When Sarah and her mother left the tattoo parlor, the sun was setting – the days were so short this time of year. Sarah looked at the trees – evergreens, mostly – silhouetted in black against the orange-pink sky. In the cold car, Sarah tried to shrink into herself, make herself as small as possible and touch as little as possible. The tattoo felt sticky – sticky and sort of scratchy – and Sarah wondered if the dressing would freeze to it. The other Sarah had left a message on her cell phone: "They're sending Charlie O'Hallahan down to get Cody. Tomorrow morning, early – if the weather's okay. I just – I thought you should know. I almost said I thought you might like to know, but that's not exactly – I mean – I'm just really sorry. About Cody. I'll see you at school."

Sarah thought – she couldn't help it – about Cody's body, how it would look when they pulled him out. She wondered if he'd look like himself. She touched the gauze pad over her tattoo and tried to remember the way it had felt when he wrote on her – the point of the pen, his little finger on her skin.

"Marcia, I strongly recommend that you do not...yes, I know. But I don't think you're gonna want to be there when we...

Still, I... Yes, we talked to the EPA, and... right. They want us to get the crane in... well, I didn't think it was an option before. I know, but... I KNOW, but... Well, if the EPA wants us to pull the whole car out, that's what... I was just worried about the diver, Marcia, not... I know. See you tomorrow, I guess...okay. Try to get some sleep. Goodnight."

Part Six: It All Falls Apart

It was snowing again the ground crunched under marcias boots as she shifted back and forth phil was still in the car he didnt want to watch he didnt understand why marcia wanted to my baby she thought my baby and she thought about once when he was two blond hair big eyes and he fell in her sisters pool he was a good swimmer she thought he loved the water how strange that it would be like this charlie the diver was underwater and then he came up and marcia assumed he had clipped the cable onto the car like they said he would onto the front of the car next to the dent where she ran into the light post at the supermarket god shed loved that car and why was she thinking that and why were her feet cold how could she feel or think anything besides my son my son and it seemed like a long time before the sound of machinery the crane pulling back phil coming to stand behind her and the ice cracking around the car her car as the front bumper came up and she didnt want to look and she couldnt help but look and the silence then the murmuring as they all realized he wasnt

there he wasnt at the wheel was he in the back no no he wasnt
he wasnt anywhere and marcia didnt feel the gravel mixed
with snow on her knees through her pants but she saw the
scrapes later

· THANK YOU ·

To everyone at Texture Press: Susan Smith Nash, Valerie Fox, and Arlene Ang, for a wonderful experience. To my mentors: Rebecca Brown and the late Constance Hunting. To all my writing groups, especially the Postcard Fiction Collaborative, led by Lyle Rosdahl, and The Band: Genevieve Betts, Marshall Warfield, and Joshua Isard. To Elaine Johanson for her endless encouragement. To the Port Townsend Writers' Conference and all my friends there, especially Jim Churchill-Dicks, Philip Shaw, Sonya Dunning, Kristen Blanton, Charisse Flynn, Eric Greenwell, Jeff Eisenbrey, and DD Wigley. To Sam Ligon, Lynn Levin, and Jordan Hartt for reading the manuscript and saying such beautiful things about it. To the Goddard College MFA program. To my long-time friends Shannon Webster, Susan Gillan, and Patricia Patterson. To my Bonnaroo buddies, and especially to Jerry Holthouse for his last-minute cover advice. To the Philadelphia music community. To Fergie's Pub. To my chosen families, the Hardisons and Alexanders. To my late grandparents, especially my grandmother Dora Stoutenberg and my grandfather Denis Thorpe, for strongly encouraging me to keep writing. To my aunt Betty Stoutenberg for her example of how to live a creative life and for always being willing to "play" with a new project. To my brother Tim, and especially to my parents, Geoff and Carol, who have never wavered in their support.

· ACKNOWLEDGEMENTS ·

The epigraph was published in *escarp*.

"Port Townsend" was published in *5x5*.

"Offshore Winds" was published in *Kahini Magazine*.

"On Vacation" and "Starting Over" were published in *Conversations Across Borders*.

"And the Future Is", "Adolescence," "The Bridesmaid," "Apnea," "Manmade," "Pareidolia," "Stealing Signs," and "Wild Like Fire" were written for the *Postcard Fiction Collaborative*. "Manmade" also appears in the anthology *Shale: Extreme Fiction for Extreme Conditions*.

"A Clean Break" was published in *Puckerbrush Review* and *The 33rd*, Drexel University's student/faculty publication.

"House of Tea" and "Cities" were published in *Press 1*.

"William Tell" was published in *Painted Bride Quarterly*.

"Punctuation" was published in *Per Contra* and *The 33rd*.

Note: Several story titles are enclosed in quotation marks, referring to song titles.

· ABOUT THE AUTHOR ·

Elizabeth Thorpe's short stories and essays have appeared in *Per Contra*, *Painted Bride Quarterly*, *5x5*, *Puckerbrush Review*, and *escarp*, among others. She teaches writing at Drexel University and in the University of the Arts Pre-College program. She edits a literary magazine called *Press 1* and does one-on-one editing sessions at the Port Townsend Writers' Conference every summer. She is a live music reviewer and photographer for Brookladelphia, a Philadelphia/Brooklyn music website, and she earned her MFA in Fiction from Goddard College. She lives in Philadelphia.